For Hannah, Elizabeth, and Oliver

MUNACHAR & MANACHAR
An Irish Story

as told by
Joseph Jacobs
with
pictures by
Anne Rockwell

Thomas Y. Crowell Company 🐾 *New York*

T 405007

A NOTE ABOUT THE STORY

In his preface to the first edition of Celtic Fairy Tales, Joseph
Jacobs wrote:

"...Ireland began to collect her folk-tales almost as early as any
country in Europe.... I have laid down the rule to include only tales
that have been taken down from Celtic peasants ignorant of English....

"While I have endeavoured to render the language of the tales
simple and free from bookish artifice, I have not felt at liberty to
re-tell the tales in the English way. I have not scrupled to retain a
Celtic turn of speech, and here and there a Celtic word, which I have
not explained within brackets—a practice to be abhorred of all good
men. A few words unknown to the reader only add effectiveness and
local colour to a narrative...."

Nevertheless, some readers may be glad to be told the meanings of
some unfamiliar words in this story: a gad is a rope woven of pliable
willow strips; a rod is a reed or willow; and a flag is a whetstone for
sharpening axes and knives.

A. R.

There once lived a Munachar and a Manachar a long time ago, and it is a long time since it was, and if they were alive now, they would not be alive then. They went out together to pick raspberries, and as many as Munachar used to pick, Manachar used to eat. Munachar said he must go look for a rod to make a gad to hang Manachar, who ate his raspberries every one...

and he came to a rod.

"What news today?" said the rod.

"It's my own news I'm seeking. Going looking for a rod, a rod to make a gad, a gad to hang Manachar, who ate my raspberries every one."

"You will not get me," said the rod, "until you get an axe to cut me."

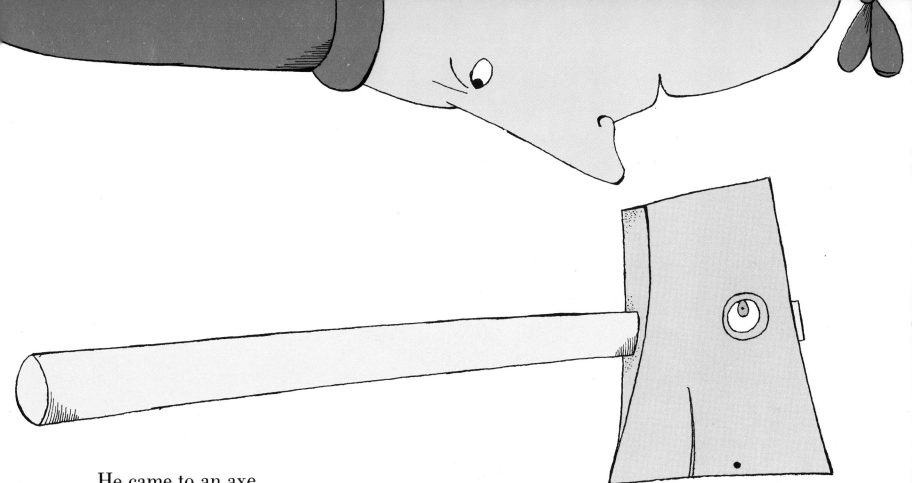

He came to an axe.

   "What news today?" said the axe.

   "It's my own news I'm seeking. Going looking for an axe, an axe to cut a rod,
a rod to make a gad, a gad to hang Manachar, who ate my raspberries every one."

   "You will not get me," said the axe, "until you get a flag to edge me."

He came to a flag.

"What news today?" said the flag.

"It's my own news I'm seeking. Going looking for a flag, a flag to edge an axe, an axe to cut a rod, a rod to make a gad, a gad to hang Manachar, who ate my raspberries every one."

"You will not get me," said the flag, "till you get water to wet me."

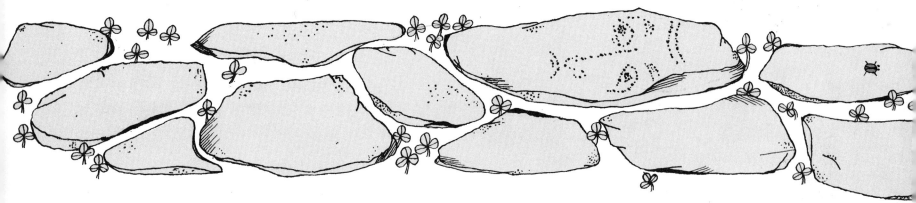

He came to some water.

"What news today?" said the water.

"It's my own news I'm seeking. Going looking for water, water to wet a flag, a flag to edge an axe, an axe to cut a rod, a rod to make a gad, a gad to hang Manachar, who ate my raspberries every one."

"You will not get me," said the water, "until you get a deer who will swim me."

He came to a deer.

"What news today?" said the deer.

"It's my own news I'm seeking. Going looking for a deer, a deer to swim water, water to wet a flag, a flag to edge an axe, an axe to cut a rod, a rod to make a gad, a gad to hang Manachar, who ate my raspberries every one."

"You will not get me," said the deer, "until you get a hound who will hunt me."

He came to a hound.

"What news today?" said the hound.

"It's my own news I'm seeking. Going looking for a hound, a hound to hunt a deer, a
deer to swim water, water to wet a flag, a flag
to edge an axe, an axe to cut a rod, a rod to
make a gad, a gad to hang Manachar, who ate
my raspberries every one."

"You will not get me," said the hound,
"until you get a bit of butter to put in my
claw."

He came to some butter.

"What news today?" said the butter.

"It's my own news I'm seeking. Going looking for butter, butter to go in the claw of a hound, a hound to hunt a deer, a deer to swim water, water to wet a flag, a flag to edge an axe, an axe to cut a rod, a rod to make a gad, a gad to hang Manachar, who ate my raspberries every one."

"You will not get me," said the butter, "until you get a cat who shall scrape me."

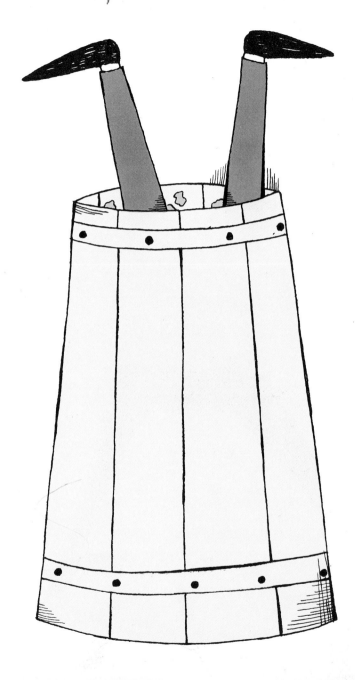

He came to a cat.

"What news today?" said the cat.

"It's my own news I'm seeking. Going looking for a cat, a cat to scrape butter, butter to go in the claw of a hound, a hound to hunt a deer, a deer to swim water, water to wet a flag, a flag to edge an axe, an axe to cut a rod, a rod to make a gad, a gad to hang Manachar, who ate my raspberries every one."

"You will not get me," said the cat, "until you get milk which you will give me."

He came to a cow.

"What news today?" said the cow.

"It's my own news I'm seeking. Going looking for a cow, a cow to give me milk, milk I will give to a cat, a cat to scrape butter, butter to go in the claw of a hound, a hound to hunt a deer, a deer to swim water, water to wet a flag, a flag to edge an axe, an axe to cut a rod, a rod to make a gad, a gad to hang Manachar, who ate my raspberries every one."

"You will not get milk from me," said the cow, "until you bring me a whisp of straw from those threshers yonder."

He came to the threshers.

"What news today?" said the threshers.

"It's my own news I'm seeking. Going looking for a whisp of straw from you to give to a cow, a cow to give me milk, milk I will give to a cat, a cat to scrape butter, butter to go in the claw of a hound, a hound to hunt a deer, a deer to swim water, water to wet a flag, a flag to edge an axe, an axe to cut a rod, a rod to make a gad, a gad to hang Manachar, who ate my raspberries every one."

"You will not get any whisp of straw from us," said the threshers, "until you bring us the makings of a cake from the miller over yonder."

He came to the miller.

"What news today?" said the miller.

"It's my own news I'm seeking. Going looking for the makings of a cake which I will give the threshers, the threshers to give me a whisp of straw, a whisp of straw I will give to a cow, a cow to give me milk, milk I will give to a cat, a cat to scrape butter, butter to go in the claw of a hound, a hound to hunt a deer, a deer to swim water, water to wet a flag, a flag to edge an axe, an axe to cut a rod, a rod to make a gad, a gad to hang Manachar, who ate my raspberries every one."

"You will not get any makings of a cake from me," said the miller, "till you bring me the full of that sieve of water from the river over there."

He took the sieve in his hand and went over to the river, but as often as ever he would stoop and fill it with water, the moment he raised it the water would run out of it again, and sure, if he had been there from that day till this, he never could have filled it.

A crow went flying by him, over his head. "Daub! daub!" said the crow.

"My blessings on you, then," said Munachar, "but it's the good advice you have."

And he took the red clay that was by the brink,
and he daubed it to the bottom of the sieve...

until all the holes were filled.

And then the sieve held the water,

and he brought the water to the miller,

FLOUR

and the miller gave him the makings of a cake,

and he gave the makings of a cake to the threshers,

and the threshers gave him a whisp of straw,
and he gave the whisp of straw to the cow,

the milk he gave to the cat,

the cat scraped the butter,

the butter went into the claw of the hound,

and the cow gave him milk,

the hound hunted the deer,
the deer swam the water,
the water wet the flag,
the flag sharpened the axe,
the axe cut the rod,

and the rod made a gad, and when he had it
ready to hang Manachar...

he found that Manachar had BURST!